CW01080748

My Book
Of
Short
Stories.

COPYRIGHTS FOR THE CONTENTS OF
THIS BOOK BELONG TO

M. POULSON, FERGUSON.

JANUARY 2011

CONTENTS.

POEM.

SPRINGS SHOUT.

THE SLEEPING TREES BEGIN TO STIR

AND SQUIRRELS LEAPFROG THROUGH

THE FIR,

IT'S SPRING AND BIRDS HAVE
FINISHED RESTING,

BUDS START POPPING AND GREEN
SHOOTS SPROUT

LEAVES AND FLOWERS SPREAD ROUND
ABOUT

IT'S SPRING AND BIRDS ARE BUSY

NESTING

NEW LIFE IS HERE THERE IS NO

DOUBT

SO ENJOY THE YOUNG ONES JOYOUS
SHOUT

IT'S SPRING AND BIRDS HAVE
FINISHED NESTING.

My first story tells of how a childish
vow of vengeance can be carried on
throughout their lifetime, waiting
patiently for a time to repay.

_____

IF I HAVE TO LIVE UNTIL
I AM 100 YEARS OLD.

_____

As the lightning bolt flashed over the
troubled sky and the thunder roared
mightily, seemingly attempting to burst
open the leaden grey clouds, the sudden
downpour sent the bunch of girls
dashing from the school playground into
the nearest shelter. Their skipping
rope lay abandoned amongst the growing
puddles scattered over the rough
playing area.

It was the year 1920 and the pupils of
Gorebridge primary school were getting
used to the normality of peace from
war.

As they crowded together in the little
shelter their shrieks, squeals and
laughter drowned out the late summer
thunder storm.

From somewhere in a corner the
struggling singing of 'Happy Birthday'
broke out. The focus was on two girls,
one small and one tall being given
their customary 'birthday dumps'. Both
were ten years old that day.

As the girls excitedly mingled
together, the smaller girl clutched
tightly,a sepia photograph wrapped
carefully in newspaper.

The tall girl's turn for her
ceremonial back slapping by her friends
began to the shouted counts, 'One-two-
three---' and when they reached the
magic number, 'ten' , they all shouted
'happy birthday Alice'.

9

In the struggle Alice's red woollen
scarf which was loosely tied around her
neck was pulled off.

Amongst the high pitched squalor a
shrill excited voice piped up above
the rest.

'Alice has a dirty neck. Alice has a
dirty neck.'

All the other girls joined in the
chant and the mortified Alice screamed
in defence. 'It's not dirty, it's a
birth mark. I was born with it.'

And she launched herself at the girl
who started it all. Her birthday
sharing friend , Little Mary.

Grabbing hold of Mary's paper covered
photo she frantically tore it into
little bits and scattered the pieces
into the air.

At that same moment, the thunder
roared loudly over the muddy sky as if
sharing the anger felt in the shelter.

Silence -, then a shrill high pitched
scream and little Mary sank to the
ground after the torn pieces of her
photo.

'My Dad' she wailed. 'You've torn my
Dad's photo to pieces.'

All merriment amongst the girls had
ceased.

'You have destroyed my photo of my
Dad.' she was sobbing heavily. 'My Dad
was killed in the war and this photo
was my only remembrance of him.'

She scrambled about on her knees
amongst the feet of her friends
collecting the remains of her treasured
picture. Some of the other girls joined
her.

With all the fragments stuffed into

her coat pocket, little Mary placed
herself truculently in front of Alice
and staring hard into her now grey
white face, made her this promise.

'I will get you back Alice Thompson
for destroying my Dad's photo.' and
with heavy sob, added. 'This is my
promise to you,' and pointing a finger
into Alice's face, 'If I have to live
until I am one hundred years old I will
somehow get you back.'

Just then the school bell rang.
Playtime was over and the now quiet
girls retreated to their classrooms.
The rain poured heavily from the low
worried looking clouds and the rasping
thunder echoed through the empty
shelter.

============

The over weight Matron organised her
little army of nurses and care workers
with military precision. Carefully they
arranged the comfortable little lounge
with flowers and bunting. The floral
red carpet had just been vacuum cleaned
and shampooed. A fresh set of gold
velvet curtains hung smartly on the big
bay window that overlooked a vast lawn
with little pockets of flowered gardens
scattered around, each with a wooden
bench seat. Truly inviting for someone
seeking relaxation with nature.

Only, today wasn't suitable for that.
Thunder was roaming about in the gloomy
distance, but getting ever nearer. The
rain clouds hung like pregnant grey
water filled plastic bags ready to
disgorge their contents on the watchers
waiting below. Lightning flashes weakly
lit up the enclosing gloom.

Safe from and not particularly
concerned about the weather, the
elderly ladies of High Grove house
retirement home finished breakfast and
gathering into two's and three's slowly
drifted out of the dining room into the

wide blue carpeted passage way that formed a continuous circle round the interior of the nursing home.

Two old ladies turned in the opposite direction to the rest and shuffled their way slowly towards a small settee that directly faced the main entrance. The small frail lady eased her walking frame carefully in front of her whilst her friend who would have been much taller but for her badly bent body, balanced her weight unsteadily on two walking sticks. Stiffly they lowered themselves into the settee and stared at the door. This was their daily practice since they met two years ago at this home.

The big glass doors looked out into the car park, but this morning, everything was quiet. To the right of the doors was the reception desk and to the left was Matrons office.

'What day is it?' the tall one asked, still leaning forward on her sticks even though she was seated.

'Don't know.' came her friends reply.

'I think it's about time for my birthday.' this was accompanied by a severe tap with one of her sticks on the carpeted floor.

'Don't know.' came her friends reply.

'I'll be one hundred soon.' the big one stated staring at a stain on the carpet.

'Don't know.' her friend replied again.

'Get a card from the queen when you're a hundred.' again tapping the floor harder this time.

'Don't know.' the small lady was absently staring through the window at the outside world.

12

'Been hanging on for that card.' she tapped the floor excitedly with both sticks then adding as if just remembering, 'from the Queen.'

'Don't know.' came the same reply.

'What do you know?' She bent her head over trying to look sideways at her friend, 'I've forgotten your name.'

'Mary.' It was whispered as if were a secret.

'Ah yes May. I've been looking forward to that,May.' She paused as the postman rang the outside bell.

'Waited a hundred years to get my card from the Queen.'

The outside door opened and the postman entered. A few cheery words with the receptionist and he left leaving a pile of letters on her desk.

'Think I'll go now.' the bent old lady grunted as she tried to get to her feet.

'Wait I'll give you a hand Alice.' the receptionist shouted to the struggling woman.

'I'm going to my room now.' she said as she accepted the offer of help. And off they went.

Mary,now alone rose to her feet and shuffling her walking frame made her way over to the receptionist's desk where she began searching through the pile of letters. Selecting one she stuffed it down the front of her blouse,slowly turned and wandered off to her own room.

That afternoon the Matron gathered her staff together once more into the lounge. 'You all know that today is a special occasion. Not only do we have one resident celebrating her one

centenary birthday we have two. Mary
and Alice.' she said this with great
pride, thrusting out her ample bosom as
if was through her personal care and
attention that they had reached such an
age.

'As you all know Mary and Alice have
no living relations so we will have to
take their place and make them feel
special.' the Matron clapped her hands
as if the meeting was over, but--- it
wasn't. 'Bring everyone in now girls.'
she commanded raising her right arm and
flourished it above her head as if
leading an attack. The staff wandered
out to mumbled moans.

'Grumpy old pair.'

 'They won't appreciate all this, you
know.'

 'They don't know what day it is never
mind how old they are.'

 Soon, well nearly soon, they had most
of their elderly charges seated around
the lounge.

 At one end all by themselves, Mary and
Alice were sitting side by side on a
long settee.

 Alice, still leaning forward on her
sticks, looked puzzled at the amount of
staff around her.

 Mary sat demurely looking into space.

 'Ladies, ladies.' shouted the Matron
hopping about excitedly. 'Two special
birthdays to celebrate today. Mary and
Alice are one hundred years old today.
Isn't that great?' she bounced her
chubby body around in front
                        1o
of the sleepy, disinterested group of
elderly inmates, ignoring a shout of
'Shoot them' from someone behind her.

 'We have two cakes.' she said

dramatically pointing to a trolley
being wheeled in bearing enormous
candle blazing icing covered birthday
cakes.

The elderly residents interest turned
to fear at the terrifying sight of so
many flames. Some screamed, some
clapped, but most just stared, open
mouthed.

Trying to get everyone into the party
spirit the Matron began singing 'Happy
Birthday'

It started off raggedly and finished
raggedly.

'And now ladies, the moment we have
all been waiting for.' The perspiring
official proclaimed waving two fancy
envelopes above her head.

'Oh get on with it woman.' Alice
growled impatiently.

'Two cards from the Queen.' she slid a
card out of it's envelope and declared
with much pomp.' This one is for Mary
wishing her a very happy one
hundredth birthday.'

A few of the staff clapped as she
handed the card to Mary who looked at
it vaguely and muttered, 'I don't
know.'

'Now the other card is for Alice who
is also one hundred years old today.

Someone from a corner shouted again,
'Shoot the batty old bitch.'

The Matron poked her fat fingers into
the envelope, then a puzzled look
spread over her face as she pulled out
a card with the torn remnants of an old
photo of a young man in uniform stuck
to it like a jig-saw. Also from
the envelope poured out the Queens
birthday card to Alice torn into small
pieces and scattered themselves all

over the carpet.

Alice let out a scream ,'My card, my birthday card from the queen. What have you done with it you silly woman?'

'Alice I'm so sorry.' Spluttered the Matron. ' I didn't know.' she didn't know what to do.

Little Mary, a huge smile on her face, got up unsteadily to her feet, and balancing on her frame quietly proclaimed.

'Ninety years ago-.' just then a dramatic peel of thunder punctuated her speech .'-a certain girl tore up a very special, prized possession of mine. My only photo of my father who was killed in the first world war. I swore then that if I had to live until I was a hundred years old I would get even. I have now.'
The room was hushed, everyone was staring at little quiet Mary.

The silence was broken by the Matron. 'How did you know it was Alice after ninety years Mary?'

'By her dirty neck.' Mary replied, smiling and pointing to Alice's birthmark.

Everyone turned to looked at Alice's neck, too stunned to say anything.

The thunder outside grumbled into silence.
Mary, balancing with one hand on her walking
frame pulled from under her blouse with the other, a card, and handing it to Alice said quietly. 'After ninety years Alice, how could I be so cruel. I just wanted to see the look of
horror on your face. Here is your birthday card from the queen.'
                    The end.

SUMMERTIME TALK.

IF PLANTS COULD TALK WHAT WOULD THEY
SAY?

DO YOU THINK THEY WOULD GRUMBLE ABOUT
THE TYPE of DAY?

WE'RE NOT LIKE HUMANS SAYS THE LOVELY
ROSE.

WE ACCEPT WITH PLEASURE WHATEVER GOES.

US ASTERS DAZZLE IN THE SUN,

SHOWING OFF OURCOLOURS IS SUCH FUN.

BENDING GRACEFULLY OUR SPIKY LEAVES

WE LILIES ENJOY A REFRESHING BREEZE.

IF PLANTS COULD TALK THEY'D MAKE IT
PLAIN

THEY ALL LOVE THE PRECIOUS RAIN.

WE'RE NOT LIKE HUMANS WE'LL REPEAT
AGAIN

WE ACCEPT THE DAY AND DON'T COMPLAIN.

MY SECOND STORY is about frustration
and how to skilfully work your way
around it. Try to imagine the scene of
a married couple preparin to go on
holiday.

THE NAKED TRUTH.

'Are you going to be in the toilet
much longer Tom?' Jill shouted from the
bedroom where she was squeezing clothes
into a big suitcase.

'Nearly finished dear.' Tom shouted
back, briefly taking the toothbrush
from his mouth to answer her.

'Are you going to tell me where we are
going darling?' She was holding two
dresses in front of her as she stood
before a full length mirror.

'I told you it is a surprise, love.'
Came the reply.

'Yes I know Tom, but if I knew where we
were going I would know what to take
with me.' Jill wheezed as she lifted
her big make up box from the floor and
dumped it on the bed.

'I told you Jill that you do not need
to take very much for this holiday.'

  Tom entered the room carrying his
toilet bag.

'Don't be ridiculous, of course I'll
need lots of things to change into.'

  Half of the contents of the make-up
box was scattered over the bed and she
was sifting through bottles, boxes and
tubes.

'You are not going to take all that
rubbish, are you?' Tom stood with his
hands on his hips as he watched her

throw everything back into the make-up box again.

'Of course. I need my make-up. I feel naked without it.' She whined, as she snapped the lid of her box shut.

Tom smiled inwardly, but only for a second then his mood changed. 'You don't need that

15

 muck on your face. You look pretty enough without it.' He snapped back angrily.

'Do want me to look like Mary, you know Bobs
 wife?' She said huffily. 'She never wears make-up and she should because she is quite plain looking. And she never wears any jewellery of any kind either, which is quite odd. I would not go out without my rings, bangles, necklaces and ear-rings.'

'Mary is not plain looking Jill. She really is quite pretty and she does not need make-up or adornments.' Tom didn't like when she was nasty about his friends.

'I think you need glasses dear.' Jill held up her two dresses again.' Which one do you think I should take?'

'None of them. We are going on a nice relaxing holiday and we don't need many clothes.'

Tom sighed and raised his eyebrows as he watched her stuff both dresses into the already full case.

'Now you really are being ridiculous Tom.' she rounded on him angrily.
'Are you going to give me a clue as to where we are going?' She folded her arms and glared menacingly.

'All right then.' He said in exasperation. 'We are going to an Island.' Her mouth opened in surprise and her eyes began darting to her chest of drawers.

'An Island. Oh great, which one? I will need a bathing suit. There is water there I take it dear?'

She pulled out a drawer and held various pieces of swimwear.

Tom hid a smile with his hand. 'Of course there is water. Plenty of it. It is an island for goodness sake. It is surrounded by water.'

'Of course. Sorry dear.' A handful of bikinis were stuffed into the corner of the case. 'I'll need to tell Mum where we are going in case she needs to contact us, dear.' She said as she picked up her mobile phone.

'No need.' Tom took the phone from her. 'Your Mum and Dad already know where we are going.'
'You told them where we are going but you won't tell me?' Her long fair hair swirled outwards as she turned quickly to face him.

'Well actually it was their idea to take you on holiday to this particular island. They thought it would be good for you.'

'Oh how thoughtful of them. I somehow knew it was not your idea.' Jill lowered the lid of her suitcase and heaved down on it. 'I can't get this shut.'

'Well why don't you take half the stuff out. You won't need it.' Tom lifted the lid of the case again.

'Tom really.' She glared angrily at him. 'Do you want me to go about looking like Helen and were baggy trousers and tops? Of course she needs to wear baggy clothes to hide her fat.'

'Now that is not nice Jill. Helen
wears clothes for comfort and you can't
talk about anybody being fat. You have
quite a few bulges yourself these
days.'

Jill's hands automatically went to her
ample tummy and non existing waist.

'I can't help it. It's my age.' Tears
welled up in her eyes. 'And it hurts
when you bring it up.'

'Well it is there my dear and you can
not hide it. With fashion clothes or
casual wear it is there for all to
see.'

'Lets change the subject.' She
snapped.

Tom laughed quietly. He was expecting
that. She always said that when she
was losing an argument.

'Is your case packed?' She snapped
again.

'Yes with all I need.' Tom replied.

'Any room for some of my things?' she
looked at him hopefully.

'Look, you will not need many clothes
for

 this holiday and you certainly will
not need any make-up.' He had raised
his voice but she was not listening.

   She was holding up a skimpy black
Bra. 'Do you think I will show too much
boob if I wear this?'

He snatched it from her. 'Yes way too
much.'

'Maybe you would prefer if I looked
like Kate and be flat chested?' She
was getting all huffed up
again.

'Now you are being nasty again, Jill.'
He felt his temper rising and he tried
hard to keep calm. Kate was his
brothers wife and he liked her a lot.

'Well she is tall and skinny and
dresses like a man. She even has her
hair cut short.'

She was on the verge of crying now and
her bottom lip quivered.

'Kate is an executive and dresses
smartly to suit her position and I
would not say she was skinny. She
exercises a lot to keep herself slim
and toned. Quite statuesque I'd say.'

She was not listening now. 'I must
visit the toilet before we go. Would
you mind shutting the case for me. I
can't manage.' and off she stormed.

   Tom quickly grabbed half the clothes
from the case and stuffed them under
the bed. Then he closed the lid of the
case and placed it near the door ready
to go.

'Don't be long.' He shouted. 'We
should be on our way. I don't want to
get caught in traffic and we have a
boat to catch.'

'I'm ready.' She came storming into
the room and grabbed her make-up case
and massive handbag. 'So we are not
flying, we are going by boat?' It
sounded more like a statement than a
question.

'Yes that's right.' Tom pushed her out
of the door and followed her. 'My
case,you idiot.' She gave him a
violent push back towards the door.
With a sigh he picked up the case.
'What have you got in here?' He
                    18
 groaned as he carried it to the car.
'It weighs a ton.'

23

'Stop moaning. You have always got to
moan.

       The traffic was busy but they made
good time and when they joined the
motorway north, their progress was
good.

'What direction are we going?' Jill
had lowered the back of her seat and
sprawled out. She stretched and placed
her hands behind her neck. A button
popped off her blouse and hit the
windscreen with a loud click and her
navel forced its way out of the gap.
'Does it matter which way we go?' he
took his eyes from the road for a
second and stared at the protruding
flesh. 'You have no sense of direction
anyway.'

'I'll put on some music.' Sitting up
again she grabbed some CD's.

'Please not your weird apology for
music. I can't stand that tuneless
repetitive garbage you normally play.'

Jill, ignoring him selected one and
pushed it into the CD slot. 'I think
this one is good.' She pushed the
button and then lowered herself back
onto her reclining seat. Tom glanced
sideways just as another button gave up
the struggle and parted company with
the blouse, which opened further to
reveal a tight black Bra.

 The music wailed monotonously and when
Jill joined in with her tuneless
squeaky voice, Tom leaned over and
switched it off.
'Spoil sport.' She hissed.
'Go to sleep.' He growled.

Which she did.

She slept soundly for the rest of the
journey. She did not even wake up when

they crossed the water in a small
ferry boat. In fact, Tom had to give
her a good shake to get her back into
the land of living when he parked his
car at the hotel.

'We have arrived.' He slapped the
bare flesh of her exposed tummy and she
swore at him. She was still in a
sleepy state when they entered the
bedroom and she stood at the edge of
the bed looking longingly at its
inviting comfort.

'Come on Jill, it's a lovely warm
afternoon. A fine start to our
holiday.'
Tom was shouting to her from the 'en-
suite'. Get undressed and we'll go out
and enjoy the sunshine.'

She was about to reply when there was
a sharp knock on the room door.
Holding her blouse closed with one hand
she opened the door with the other.
There was no one there, so she peeked
out into the passage. Her eyes and
mouth opened wide and she placed both
hands over her mouth to suppress a
scream. She slammed the door shut and
stood with her back to it. 'Tom. Tom
we are in the wrong place. This is not
a hotel, it's an old folks home.' Her
chest heaved violently and a boob
squeezed out of the tight black Bra.

'Calm yourself woman. This is a
hotel.' He shouted back.

She heard the en-suite door slide
open and bare feet slapping over the
cord carpeting. 'No it's not. I've
just seen two fat elderly people walk
down the passage and they were both
naked. Do you hear Tom? They were
both totally naked.' She shouted the
last part.

'It's okay Jill, they are allowed to be naked.' And he appeared before her completely naked.
A bemused look crossed her face and her hand came up and pointed to him. 'Tom you have no clothes on.'
'Well spotted dear, now get your clothes off.' A wide grin spread across his face as he walked towards her.
'Now Tom.' She held her hands up, palms facing towards him. 'Not now, this isn't the time, we have just arrived.'
He took hold of an outstretched arm and pulled her roughly to the balcony door, opened it and pushed her out. 'There now.'
He said pointing to the lush green grounds where tables and chairs were spread out around a lovely swimming pool. 'What do you see?'
Jill looked down and her hands went to her mouth and she gasped. 'Everyone is naked.'
'Well spotted again.' He lifted an arm and waved to couple sitting at a table. 'Do you see anyone you know?'
Gripping the balcony railing, she leaned over. 'Is that your sister-in-law Kate Tom?' Her finger was pointing down.
'It certainly is Jill.' He placed his gently on her shoulders.
'But she's got breasts Tom.' Her eyes were almost popping out of her head.
'Well so she has dear. I did not notice.' Gently he pulled her blouse over her shoulders and let it hand on her arms.
'And there is Bill, but who is that pretty girl with him?'

'That's Mary. You know his plain
looking wife and she still isn't
wearing make-up.' His fingers were now
unfastening her black Bra.

'And that lady standing by the pool
looks remarkably like Helen.' He
whispered into her ear. 'But she isn't
wearing baggy clothes.'

'But she has a lovely figure Tom.
Where has all her fat gone?'

'She has been working hard at the gym,
I believe, and she certainly looks
good.'

He slipped her Bra off and released her
breasts.

'But Tom, I can't go down there and mix
with them with no clothes on. I mean,
look at them and look at me.'

'How about looking at that couple over
there Jill.' He was pointing to an
elderly couple that came out of the
hotel and sat down at a table by the
pool.

   His arms were around her waist now
and his fingers were undoing the belt
holding up her expensive trousers.

'They are that fat couple I saw in the
passage Tom. They look like- -oh my--
it is.' She hesitated and blinked her
eyes several times. 'It is Mum and
Dad.'

Tom pulled her trousers and pants down
in one swift downward movement and
stood up. 'It is Mum and Dad Jill.
They have been coming to this Nudist
camp holiday Hotel for years. This
year we are all their guests. It's an
anniversary of something. I don't know
what.' and putting his mouth to her
ear, whispered.

27

'And now you are nearly naked as well,
how do you feel?'

'Nearly naked. I am naked Tom and I
think I feel quite free.' She
giggled.

'Not quite Jill, remove your adornments
and wash off your make-up and then you
will be completely
naked and completely free. Then we can
go down and meet the rest.' He took
her hand and led her indoors.

THE END.

POEM.

AUTUMN WHISPER.

IT CREEPS UP FAST WHEN SUMMERS PAST

THE DAYLIGHT HOURS JUST DO NOT LAST

CHILL WINDS BLOW AND MAKE US GASP

WHISPER, IT'S AUTUMN.

THE LEAVES TURN RED AND THEN THEY FALL

A GOLDEN CARPET FOR ONE AND ALL

LEAF MOULD FOR GARDENERS, I HEAR YOU
CALL

WHISPER IT'S AUTUMN

THE GLORIOUS MANTLE OF DECIDIOUS LEAVES

DEPART FOREVER FROM THOSE GLORIOUS
TREES

COME BACK NEXT YEAR, OH PLEASE, OH
PLEASE

WHISPER IT'S AUTUMN.

——————————

WE ARE ALL GUILTY OF

FORGETFULNESS.

AND THIS IS A TYPICAL STORY,

I FORGOT.

'Have you seen my glasses Bert?'
Mabel walked about with a
magazine in her hands as she
looked in all the likely places
for her spectacles.
 'You are always looking for
 your specs.
Can't you remember where you
last used them.'
Her husband sighed as he glanced
 around.

 'I was sitting in that chair
 there.'
She pointed to an easy chair
 that was opposite to Bert.
'Then that is where you will

 find them.'

 He sank his overweight body back
down into his own chair.
 Mabel lifted a scatter cushion.
'Yes you are right love, they are
 here.' She picked them up and
 tried to straighten a bent leg.
'I must get them repaired.' She
 muttered to herself.
 'You keep saying that Mabel.
 you keep saying that.' Bert
 held up his paper to read again.
 'Yes I know but I keep
31

forgetting.' His wife grunted as
she sat down. With her glasses
on she began to flick through
the pages of her magazine as her
husband distantly remarked.'
'You are always forgetting.
They were startled when the
phone wrung.
Bert sighed and hauled himself
out of his comfortable seat and
shuffled to a small table on
which the phone lay. He picked
it up and shouted. 'Hello.' and
listened. 'Oh it's you Edith.'
He said quieter. 'What do you
want?' A puzzled look crossed
his face as he listened.

'Okay Edith I'll tell her.' He
put the   phone down
                    slowly.
'That was your sister love.'
        'So I gather, what did she
        want?' Mabel was looking
interestedly at some pictures in
her magazine. Bert scratched his
balding head before answering.
'She said, when are you going to
        return the tartan skirt you
borrowed?' Mabel quickly lowered
                        her magazine.
'What tartan skirt?'

'I don't know love. Your Edith
is going bonkers I think.'
He dropped his heavy body into
his   easy chair and they both
went back to reading again.
After a short while of silence
Mabel dropped her magazine onto
her lap. 'You know Bert, the

only time I borrowed a tartan
 skirt from Edith was when we
 were teenagers and I was going
 on holiday with my friends.'
'It's a long time since you were
 a teenager Mabel.' Came the
snide remark from her grinning
husband. 'What happened to the
tartan skirt?'
Mabel thought for a moment.
 'Don't know.
 Lost it I think.'
 'Why is she bringing this up now
 then.'
Bert laid down his paper and
 looked quizzically at his wife.
'I don't know. Do you think she
 is losing it Bert?' Mabel did
 not look very worried.
'Well I have always thought you
 sister was weird, love' Bert
 picked up his paper and the
 subject was closed.
  The next evening as Bert sat
 down to read his paper before
 bedtime his wife was walking
 around looking under cushions.
'Seen my glasses Bert?'
Have you tried your chair?'
He looked over his paper and
 nodded towards where she
 normally sat, a smirk was
 creeping over his face. Mabel
 shook her head and shrugged her
 shoulders.
'I have already looked. They
 are not there.'
'Have you tried your head?' His
 smirk turned into a wide grin.
Her hand went quickly to her
 head 'Ah yes. Your right love,
 they are on my head.'

She pulled them from the top of
 her head
 and straightened the bent leg
and put them on. They both
settled down to read and after a
while Bert's head dropped forward
and his eyes closed and he began
to snore. Just then, the phone
wrang and he jumped. Grumbling,
he moved his bulk to the phone
and picked it up.
 'Hello.' He shouted. 'What do
you want?' He listened. 'Oh
really. Okay I will tell her---
I said I will tell her.' He
growled angrily and slammed the
phone   down.
 'That was Edith again Mabel.'
Bert sat down shaking his head.
'She wants to know when you are
 going to pay back the ten pounds
 you borrowed from her?'
 Mabel sat up quickly. 'What ten
 pounds. Why would I borrow money
 from her. She always complains
 she has none.'
 'I know love, she is just a
 miserly old spinster.' He
 groaned loudly as he leaned back
 in his chair.
 They both began to read again,
 Edith forgotten.
 Then a cry from Mabel startled
 Bert 'I did borrow ten pounds
 from Edith.'
 'Ah, so you remember dear. I
 will give her it back tomorrow.'
 Bert said as he straightened his
 paper. 'That will keep the old
 goat quiet.'
 'But Bert, it was about thirty
 years ago I borrowed the money.'
34

she stared at him, eyes wide.
'Goodness me, how could the old
miser remember that far back?'

'I'm getting worried about her
Bert.'
Mabel looked worried.
'Oh yeah. Well she's not coming
here to live, so do not even
think about it.' Bert pointed a
finger at her for effect.
The next evening the phone rang
before they had time to sit down
and read. Bert grabbed the phone
angrily. 'That will be her
again.' He growled as he yelled
into the mouthpiece. 'What do
you want now?' He listened.

'Wait I will put you over to
Mabel—I said I will put you over
to----Oh very well Edith, tell
me.' He listened for a few
moments then slammed the phone
down loudly.
'What does she want now Bert?'
Mabel stared anxiously at him.
He laughed as he spoke. 'She
said you promised to take her to
Blackpool for the September.'

'Did I? I can't remember that.
But this is only March.' Mabel
looked puzzled.
'Well did you ever promise her a
holiday.' Bert was still
laughing.
Mabel thought hard and finally.
'Oh
Bert. Surely she can't still
remember that. It's nearly
thirty years ago. I said to her
35

that if I ever won a lot of
money I would take her there for
a holiday.' She sniffed. 'It
was not even a real promise
Bert.'
 'Well the crazy fool seems to
think it was. But the real bad
news is, she is coming here
tomorrow for a visit. She says
she has a lot more scores to
settle with you.'
  The next day they prepared for
Edith's visit. Bert placed a ten
pound note by the phone, then
sat down in his easy chair by
the fire while Mabel prepared
tea. When Edith arrived Bert
answered the door.
She was standing waiting,
   leaning on her walking stick,
a big bag hung from her neck by
a long strap and she peered at
him through thick glasses.
'What took you so long. I have
arrived.'
Her lips twisted in a snarl.
 'I can see that.' Bert snapped
  impatiently. 'You'd better come
in.' He stood aside to let her
pass.

  'Oh thanks for the welcome.'
She
  snapped.
  She hobbled into the living room
and
  looked around. 'Still the
same.' She said as she ran a
finger over the polished surface
of the china cabinet and sniffed.
Then she hobbled painfully over
to Bert's chair and flopped down
36

wearily. 'Ah that's better.'

'Sit down, why don't you.'
 Bert's sarcastic remark brought
a warning glare from his wife.
 There was a long silence as
Edith stared straight into the
fireplace. Bert and Mabel looked
 at each other with raised
eyebrows.
 'Edith.' Mabel broke the
silence making her sister jump.
'Why have you decided to visit?'
 She looked startled. 'Eh. Oh
why did I come?' She rummaged in
her bag and came out with a
notebook and began flicking
through the pages until she came
to one that interested her.
 'Yes I remember now. I came
here
 because you stole my jewellery
and I want it back.' Edith
pointed a threatening finger at
her sister as she spoke.
 ' I never stole your Jewellery.
 I very seldom wear any and I
don't own much.' Mabel replied
angrily as she fiddled with the
broken leg of her glasses.
 'Yes exactly, that is why you
stole mine.' Retorted the angry
 little woman. 'You have none of
your own.'
 There was silence as Mabel
thought. 'I remember borrowing
ear rings from you when we were
teenagers.' She exclaimed as she
rubbed her ear lobes.
 'Borrow. You stole them. I
never got
them back.' Her sister stormed.

'You were always stealing my things.' Edith
looked at her book again. 'Ah yes. You even stole my
boyfriend.' She looked fiercely at Mabel.
 Bert tried to butt in. 'That's not true
 Edith---' only to be stopped abruptly. 'Oh not you Bert.'
She said with sarcasm.
'Definitely not you. Never fancied you. Too fat.' She
looked at him sideways. 'Your even fatter now.'
 'Oh thank you.' He growled.
'Why have you never mentioned these things before?'
 Edith wriggled in the chair trying to
make herself comfortable. 'You should get this chair upholstered
properly.' She grumbled, then added. 'The reason I have come
is because I am worried about your memory Mabel.' She peered
at her sister with screwed up eyes. Mabel stared back, mouth
open in surprise.
 'There is nothing wrong with my memory Edith.' She said
defensively. 'I forget where
I put my glasses and small things like that. But you are
stretching things a bit far I think.'
 'Yes.' Bert stormed. 'Look here is your ten pounds. That's
one thing settled.' He handed out the note to her which she snatched
quickly and stuffed into her bag.

'What about the interest the ten pounds would have made over thirty years?' She looked pleadingly at Bert.

Bert was deflated. 'I think you are
 being ridiculous Edith. But anyway how are you able to remember all these things now?'
 'Because I looked in my little book. I came across my old diary the other day. I used to write every thing down when I was young. See.' She held up the tatty book for Bert to read.
 'But why bring it all up now Edith?'
 Mabel asked.

 'Well dear.' She began in a softer note. 'I was worried about you.' She put her book back into her bag. 'I thought you were losing your memory so I decided to test it out.'
But why Edith?' Mabel was clearly
puzzled.

'Because you forgot my birthday last week. You never forget my birthday'

 Mabel gasped. 'Edith, I never forgot your birthday. I did send you a card. In fact Bert wrote your address on the envelope for me. Didn't you Bert?'
'Yes, that's right I---'Bert groaned. His hands clasped his head. 'Oh no.' He wailed. 'I forgot you moved to your new

house last year Edith. I must
have written your old address on
the envelope by mistake.' He
looked pleadingly at the two
women. 'I forgot.'

The end.

Poem.

Winters Silence.

The trees are bare now that
Winters here
It's cold and frosty and snow is
near
But listen, can't you hear
It's silence.
The mornings are dark and
evenings too,
Daylights short and there's a
hazy view,
But listen, can you hear it Woo?
It's silence.
The snowflakes fall and every
things white.
It helps to brighten the dreary
night
But listen, in that eerie light
There's silence.

This story starts in 1945 when I was still a boy and the war was nearing its end but rationing and shortages were very much rife. The incidents are real enough though and I write them with a certain pride.

Maybe older readers will remember and laugh.

Maybe younger readers will laugh, and remember.
I have named it.

BLACK BOXING SHORTS AND SECOND HAND FOOTBALL BOOTS.

'Mum, I have been picked to play for the school football team.' I shouted at her breathlessly. I can still feel the excitement I felt that day I had rushed home to tell Mum that I had made it into the school
under Thirteens football team.

'Oh that's good Tom, very good.' I remember her half interested reply, as she strained to turn the handle on the big mangle at the back door of our house.

'It's the final of the schools league Mum.' I persisted.

'Oh very nice Tom, that's very good.' She gasped, her cheeks red ,as a big white bed sheet squeezed out of the rollers into a big tin bath. She picked it up with red sore looking hands and with a great deal of effort shook it. It left her tired wet fingers and draped itself over the top of me.

'Mum I need new football boots.' I said angrily as I peeled the soggy sheet off my head, 'My boots are too tight for me now and I also need white football shorts.' I asked, but I knew what was coming as soon as I said it.

This was 1945. The second world war was nearing its end. My Father was in the Army and Mum and me lived with her Mum and Dad. in a small country village.

'Can't afford new boots Tom. There's a war on, you know.' That was always her answer when I wanted something.

Well I knew very well there was a war on, I was five when it started.
When Dad was conscripted into the army he tried to assure

me he wouldn't be gone long. Of course I had no idea what it was all about really, but this war thing did seem exciting to me. People were preparing for air attacks by putting blackout materials on their windows. Bomb shelters were going up in gardens and Air Raid Wardens were parading the streets at night. Sirens eerily warned of Air raids and the All clear ones sounded the welcome relief.

Staying with Gran and Granddad was fun. They had been through all this war thing before when the First World War raged. To go without things was not new to them.

'Granddad.' I shouted. He was busy digging for victory in his garden.
'I've been picked to play in the school football team for the cup final game next week.'

He leaned on his spade and smiled. 'Oh well done Tom, that's great. I'll come and watch you play.'

'But I won't be able to play Granddad, I've no football boots. I need new boots. Mum says she can't afford new boots.' I remember there were tears in my eyes when I said it.

'Oh I see lad.' He said as he wiped his forehead with a big chequered handkerchief. 'Aye, well things are quite tough these days, right enough.'

Of course I piled it on. 'I need white shorts as well, you know.' I put on a pleading look. In those days the schools only provided the football shirt and socks. You had to provide your own white shorts and boots yourself.

'We'll see what we can do Tom. You mustn't miss an opportunity like that, eh.' He said ruffling my mop of fair hair.

Granddad and I got on well together. He was my mate. I remember the nights when there was Air raids, we would stand together at the door and watch the Spitfires and Hurricanes chase enemy bombers. We could see the tracer bullets flying everywhere in black night sky. The searchlights endless probing, criss-crossing, trying to catch the enemy in their piercing yellow beams. The big guns blasting their deadly flack high into the black sky. The smell of cordite wafting in the night air.

It was in between those busy times that he would tell me about his young foot balling days. '

When I played for Arniston Thistle Bluebells, I won several medals.' He would say, and pulling a big silver hunter pocket watch from his waistcoat pocket he proudly added. 'I won this for being the player of the year in 1912.'

I was determined I was going to be a great player some day, just like him.

Then there was the night all the enemy activity was over nearby Edinburgh town and the Firth of Forth naval bases and he was recalling the time he scored a hat-trick in the cup final to win the game. I couldn't take my eyes of his whiskered face. He made everything sound exciting. Suddenly he stopped talking and pointing towards Edinburgh . 'Look at that lad.' He exclaimed.

 'There's been a direct hit on something.'

Sure enough a large angry glow lit up the darkness. A bomb had landed on a whisky bond. It was said that whisky ran down the streets like water.

Then a German bomber broke loose and headed our way chased by a Spitfire
. We watched in icy fascination as it flew overhead and a few minutes later an almighty blast struck us and sent us staggering , rattling windows and doors. A land mine had been dropped and thankfully, landed harmlessly in a field on the outskirts of the village.

To me all these things added more and more excitement to Granddad's story telling.

The day of the football match was drawing nearer and I still had no boots or shorts. 'Mum.' I tearfully appealed, as I watched her furiously trying to rub the life out of one of Granddads shirts on the scrubbing board protruding from a mass of soap suds that spilled over the edge of a large worn wooden wash tub. The smell of carbolic soap made my nose hurt. 'Mum, I will have to let someone else take my place in the football team.'

'Oh very good Tom, very good. Your father will be proud of you.' She puffed breathlessly as she shook the suds from the shirt all over me. 'Well done Tom.'

Sometimes I wondered if Mum was living on a different planet

'Oh Mum' I uttered in disgust wiping my face on my

sleeves, and went to look for Granddad.

I found him in his shed . 'Ah Tom, I have something for you my boy.' And he held up a pair of football boots. 'Your size too' He said proudly.

The boots, were of course, second hand but in good condition and they fitted just right.

'Great,' I squeaked, 'now all I need is shorts'

Granddad smiled widely. 'You better go and see Grandma then.'

She was in the kitchen ironing. An iron was stuck on the range to heat and an other iron was in her hand , furiously pummelling the creases in Granddad's long johns. She gave me a toothless grin as she said. 'Tom, you wanted boxing shorts, here you are.' And held up a pair of black silk boxing shorts. I think Mum and Grandma came from the same weird planet.

The football match was the next day, I would be able to play, but black silk boxing shorts? I would be a laughing stock. Then a crushing blow. A telegram arrived saying Dad was missing in the D-Day landings. I felt the life being sucked out of me. My Dad missing. I wouldn't be fit to play. But Granddad insisted my Dad would have wanted me to play.

I stood forlornly on the pitch surrounded by happy bouncing players in white shorts and I felt miserable, a missing Dad, second hand boots and black silk boxing shorts. I was just doing this for Granddad I tried hard to convince myself.

The first half I was terrible. My heart just wasn't in the game. I just
wanted to hear the final whistle. When the first half ended we were two goals down and when my sports teacher called me over, I thought this is it, I'm finished, but I didn't care.

'Tom' he shouted, 'your Granddad wants to see you.'

I looked round and saw him hobbling excitedly through the small crowd towards me.
'He's safe Tom.' He shouted but he was badly winded.
'Your Dads all right, they found him.' He gave me a big hug. ' Then he pushed me away gently.

'Now go and score your hat-trick lad. You can do it.'

The second half was blur. I played like I was possessed. I scored two goals so now it was a draw. I could hear Granddads voice above the rest as he roared loudly. 'Get your hat-trick Tom. You can do it.'

The opposing defence laid all their wrath on me. I was aching from numerous rough tackles and just when I broke clear with the ball in front of an empty goal mouth ,I was ruthlessly brought down. It was a penalty. I nervously placed the ball on the spot and stepped back. The gaols at that moment looked small and the keeper large. I ran towards the ball and smacked it with all the strength I could muster into the left corner. It was going good, the keeper dived, his fingers connected, but not enough. The ball slammed into the net. It was a goal. I had scored my hat-trick. Then the final whistle blew. We had won.

I was the hero of the match with my mates and they carried me high on their shoulders. I felt so proud. It was a day I would never forget. But my greatest possession to remind me of that day is the big Silver Hunter Pocket Watch my Grandfather presented me with, after the match. His own.

That was for my hat-trick he said,-- in spite of my second hand boots
and black silk boxing shorts.

The end.

/That was-

A little tale of times gone by

The touch, the feel, the wonder why

They were so real to us then, but how

Can we recall them so vividly now?

They are locked in our minds, our past ordeal

We have lived that life that's why they are real.

My next story is for dog lovers. My little white West Highland Terrier is quite a character and has a mind of his own and habitually leads me where he wants to go.

As this story shows he likes to go shopping and market days are his favourite.

MY DOG BARNEY.

His wet black button nose circled the air, sifting through the differing smells that permeated around him, ears twitching from side to side like small radar scanners and after much posturing he finally fixed his big brown eyes on a direction and off he went. The long black lead tugging at his red tartan collar and I of course had to follow.

When you own a stubborn, wilful, West Highland terrier you have no option. You know who is boss, as any owner of that lovely breed will confirm.

Through the crowds he weaved, dodging this way and that way through the discarded litter, avoiding the multitude of feet that threatened to trample him, until he reached his goal.
We were at the towns local Saturday market and he was looking for his favourite stall, the cheese stall. With unerring ease he found it. A trestle table covered with a plain white cloth and laden with a variety of different cheeses, biscuits and pickles.

The owner, a large cheery lady sporting a white straw hat over her short grey hair and wearing a blue and white striped apron emblazoned with the slogan 'I am cheesily the best' across her ample bosom, was gustily trying to out do the other traders in an effort to attract the crowds attention to her own wares. 'Come and sample my cheeses.' she bawled over and over again. 'Get your cheese and pickles here.'

Barney stood looking hopefully at her. He hopped about on his stubby, sturdy little legs excitedly trying to attract her attention. He was in luck. Her red cheeked face burst into a huge smile as she noticed him and shouted. 'I have one at home just like you,' she laughingly said, 'and he likes cheese as well.'

He sat in front of her, his little bottom twitching, his big eyes
popping, watching as she cut off a chunk of cheddar and coming round to the front of the table bent down to give

49

him his tit-bit and he gently took it from her. I watched in envy as he slowly chewed his prize, savouring every morsel. When he was finished he looked hopefully at his new found friend, once again licking his lips, his erect tail wagging from side to side. Then when he realised that no more tasty bites were forth coming and the lady had turned her attention to a paying customer, he looked up to me as if to say, it is time to go.

Before setting off, he cocked his leg against her table leg and having left his parting gift he happily and jauntily propelled his little white body to his next destination stall.

Dodging and weaving once more through the crowd of shoppers, he doggedly dragged me to a van from which fresh and cooked meats were sold. The delicious mixed beefy odours no doubt a temptation to his canine taste buds. He parked himself in front of the van's side window but here he had a more difficult time attracting attention. The counter was high and the serving assistant quite small. But a few sharp barks had the laughing girl leaning over to speak to him. 'I see you lovely boy.' She shouted and with a flick of her wrist she threw a piece of cooked ham which Barney caught quite effortlessly and quickly devoured. Then, his little pink tongue, flicking over his shiny black lips and nose he glanced upwards and gave a woof of thanks to the giggling girl.

Satisfied his shopping expedition had been successful he grabbed his lead in his mouth and with a sweep of his head dragged me out of the market place, homeward bound. But not before cocking his leg and leaving his trade mark on the vans rear wheel.

The end.

The next story is compiled from true accounts from my maternal family history and is told in flash back through the eyes of my grandfather,
Harry. I named it----

THE ROSE OF TRALEE.

/

(There were still two sailing ships anchored side by side in the harbour, their sails neatly furled. Seagulls lined the spars and everything was peaceful and still. Or nearly. A big steam powered ship ploughed its way through the coming and going of the smaller craft traffic, emitting its foul smoke into the clear blue sky, spoiling the picturesque scene of Portsmouth harbour. We stood for a few minutes in silence behind the horse drawn hearse. Just a small group of us, three men and three women.
It reminded us of when we all stood at this very same spot many years ago, all much younger but in happier circumstances.)

/

I was just eighteen, it was my first leave and I proudly marched in my new sailors uniform up to where my mother and two sisters were waiting by the harbour wall. With me were my new mates, William who came from Lancashire, Mac from Scotland and of course Michael who came from Ireland.

'Hi Mum.' I shouted as we drew near. She looked great in her long black dress, her hand holding on to her big flower bedecked hat. She liked hats, in fact Mother liked to dress well and always kept an eye on all the latest fashions.

'Let me introduce my shipmates.' I said proudly as I turned to them.
'This is William and Mac. They joined at the same time as I did, but
Michael has been in the navy since he was sixteen.'

They all shook hands. My sisters were looking very smart. I suppose I could grudgingly say quite pretty. They were younger than me and I noticed they were quite taken by my mates. Mother was a bit shy, especially when she took Michaels proffered hand. Michael of course, I remember, ever the Irish charmer holding on to my Mothers hand a bit longer than necessary and exclaiming. 'Harry, you didn't

51

tell me your Mother was beautiful.'

I like my Mother blushed a bit. I had never thought of my
Mother being beautiful. Yes a fine looking woman
perhaps, but beautiful? Just the Irish blarney I thought.

Then I stood and watched open mouthed as they all walked
away, William with Sarah and Mac with Charlotte and
Michael was still holding Mothers hand. I was left standing
alone. And that is the beginning of this story.

/(Over the harbour the seagulls screeched, swooped and
dived. The smell of soot and brine wafted in from the sea.
The tall man standing in front of the carriage, dressed in
black, a tall stove pipe hat on his head grabbed hold of the
lead horse's reins and with a clatter of hooves on the
cobbled road, set off again. We were now joined by a small
contingent of Naval ratings who walked behind the hearse
but in front of us. Slowly we walked through the narrow
street towards the cemetery,leaving behind the shouts and
clattering noise of the traders as they set up their stalls at
the harbours edge, their respectful silence now over./)

 I had been encouraged to join the navy by my
Grandfather. Rather forcefully I must state. It was for my
own good he insisted. He was a man of some standing in
the town of Aston in Birmingham and to have a wayward
grandson was not good for his image.

Yes I got into trouble quite a lot. I had a fiery temper to
match my red hair, and worse, a liking for strong drink.
Not a good mix. My mother would come to my defence
with the excuse that I did not have a fatherly figure to
guide me, my father having died when I was only six. But
Grandfather would not have any excuses. I needed
discipline, he said. The Navy would give me that and it
would make a man of me, he argued, it was either the Navy
or jail.
We could not argue with him really. He had looked after
us pretty well and living was tough for a widow with a
family. So it was off to the navy I went.

The training was tough at first in those old sailing ships,
but looking back, I really enjoyed it and went on to be a
brass fitter in the more modern steam ships. But I still had
my quick temper and therefore suffered the wrath of Naval
punishment on many occasions. And I remember,
Michael, my self appointed father figure saving me from a
lot of grief on many other occasions.

(The procession stopped at the graveyard gates, the ornaments on the horses harnesses jangled as they pranced impatiently. We could smell the warm steam from their backs as it drifted back towards us. The sailors lifted the coffin from the hearse and carrying it aloft walked slowly up the path towards the open grave. The priest walked solemnly in front.
The rest of us followed. Somewhere in the distance children laughed and shouted as they played.)

Mother moved down to Portsmouth in 1891 to live permanently. She rented a house at 8 Pimlico Place Landport. I could not at the time understand why she did this but she soon opened up her little furniture shop and she was joined later by my sisters. Suddenly we were a family again. Well more than a family really, because my mates were there visiting more often than I was.

They were good times. Many happy gatherings. Michael was a good singer and kept us all entertained with his rendering of Irish songs. His favourite was 'The Rose of Tralee.' and many times a tear would enter his eyes as he sang it. But we all laughed at Mothers embarrassment when he would get down on one knee in front of her when he came to that part of the song, 'and twas there I loved Mary the Rose of Tralee.' Of course he would substitute Harriet, my Mothers name, for Mary. She would blush and protest when we kidded her about her young man.

'Don't be silly,' she would shout, 'he is much too young for me.' Or. 'I am old enough to be his mother.' But she always looked forward to his visits.

Other things were also happening. Sarah and William were spending a lot of time together and Mac and Charlotte were showing more than a little interest in each other.

At times I felt rather lonely.

(The peaty smell of the damp fresh soil permeated the air as we took our places by the graveside, the sailors slowly lowered the coffin into the freshly dug hole. Standing back they took their hats off and lowered their heads whilst the priest began the service with a prayer. Someone nearby sobbed softly.)

In the year 1892 a big sea exercise was organised by the Admiralty to take place off the coast of Libya. I was a junior crew member on the HMS Victoria, the Admirals ship.

Mac and William were crew members of the HMS Camperdown and Michael was chief stoker on the HMS Niade, a supply ship. These ships left a week before the Victoria and consequently the crew members of the Victoria were given a few days shore leave. What happened next was to have a dramatic affect on my life.

I had been trouble free for a long time, purely through the influence of Michael, but he was at sea and I had shore leave and I got drunk and caused a disturbance. Well more than that. I had assaulted some policemen, was arrested and jailed.
The Victoria sailed without me. Sadly it never returned. It is said in the course of the exercise the Admiral gave the wrong command causing a fatal collision between the Camperdown and the Victoria. The Victoria sank. There were very few survivors.

Back in Portsmouth people crowded the gates to the Admirals offices seeking news of their loved ones. My Mother was among them and her heartbreak was shared with hundreds of others when the names of those who perished were posted. The Admirals name headed the list. My name was amongst the rest.
Mother did not know I was in prison

(A few other people had gathered around the graveside and their added voices gave extra volume as we sang together 'Abide with me'. The sun was now high in a cloudless sky. A peaceful breeze gently swept the short green grass around the graves bringing with it the sweet smell of an unknown shrub. It was a good day for a funeral.)

Two days after the Victoria disaster I was released from prison and I went straight to see my Mother. I was angry that no one had told her I was alive. Mother was in her shop. .She was a cane chair maker like my Grandfather and her two sisters. She was making herself busy when I stepped into her workshop. I will never forget that sad lost look on her face as she weaved canes into shape. Tears were welled up in her eyes. A look of disbelief flooded her face as she recognised me. 'Harry. Is it really you?' She seemed to move in slow motion as she ran towards me.
'Harry, how?' Tears rolled down her cheeks. I laughed as I hugged her tightly. 'I'm alive Mother. My quick temper saved my life. I've been in jail. I was not on the Victoria

when it went down.'

'Oh I thought I had lost you son.' She clung to me tightly, fearing to let me go.

That was a happy occasion in a dark time, I lost a lot of mates.

Not long after that I was persuaded to leave the navy, by the navy.

In 1894, William and Sarah were married and Michael continued to see more of Mother. She still insisted that there was nothing in it, that they both enjoyed each others company and nothing more. In 1898 Mac left the navy and went back to Scotland to live taking Charlotte with him. That same year Sarah had a son and I met Louise who came from Devon. We set up home at 3 Pimlico Place, neighbours of Mother.

In March 1900 Louise gave birth to our daughter, Sarah, and William and sister Sarah were planning to join Charlotte and Mac for a new life in Scotland. And Michael made it clear he wanted to marry Mother. She still insisted she was too old for him, but he persisted.
 'Look Mum,' we argued, 'what is age when you love each other, and we know how you feel about each other.'

'Yes I do have feelings for him and I do enjoy his company. I admit that, but I am eighteen years older than him. Michael is only thirty.'
She added. 'Maybe I am just old fashioned.'

Well old fashioned or not, Sarah came up with the answer and a wedding was arranged in the local church, planned for the 4th of September 1900. There was no escape now for Mother.

There was only a few gathered that day. Mother looked good in her wedding outfit. A long dark green dress with puffed up sleeves and a white starched bib. A big fancy hat to match. Mother did not spare the expense to dress well for her wedding day.

She looked great. To Michael of course, she was his beautiful rose.
Michael himself looked very smart in his uniform and with his service ribbons and a typical sailors handsome beard he looked much more mature than his thirty years. Mother by contrast looked charmingly young, --or was that just the magic of the day.

Funny thing was, magic or not, on the marriage certificate, Mother had lost eight years off her age and Michael had gained six. But who was going to notice a little thing like that?

As the years rolled by, Louise and I with our now three girls joined my mates in Scotland. We had served together when we were young.

Joined together by marriage and we were now destined to live and work together when we were older.

Mother and Michael continued to live in Portsmouth and when he retired from the navy he joined the naval reserves. Consequently when the war broke out in 1914 he was recalled for duty. It was when he was returning from a training course at London docks he collapsed at the railway station. He had suffered a fatal heart attack. He was only forty five.

(The handful of soil made a soft thud as it landed on the coffin lid.
The priest ended the service with a prayer and somewhere in the distance, as if rehearsed, a ship's siren sounded. A tribute to a sailor. William, Mac, Sarah, Charlotte and myself began to sing in shaky tones, The Rose of Tralee. Our tribute to our friend, shipmate and--stepfather Michael. A tear trickled down Mothers face when we faced her as we sang the words 'His rose of Tralee.')

The end.

The following story I felt I had to include. It is a sort of branch of
the previous tale, but never-the-less still true in content. I have
named it simply-----

THE LIFE OF HARRIET.

The sun rose slowly over the ridge of trees that bordered the long green lawn facing the old grey stone building of the nursing home. A warm summer breeze drifted through the open window of the bedroom, carrying with it the heavy sweet scent of the honeysuckle that clung to the outer walls.

The room was sparsely furnished. The plain blue painted walls had no pictures or mirrors hanging on them and the lino floor covering was faded and worn, just like the old threadbare carpet that lay neatly in front of a single bed. Nice clean white freshly laundered sheets lay on top next to a single pillow. An old radio on the small bedside cabinet was playing soft nostalgic music that drifted over to the grey haired elderly lady seated in an old worn easy chair. In one shaky hand she held her spectacles, in the other a few faded photographs. Tears was in her eyes.

The room door opened quietly and a young cheery faced nurse entered carrying a cup of tea with a biscuit balanced on its saucer, which she laid down on a small table by the easy chair. 'How are you feeling today Harriet?' She greeted her patient with a smile and a little hug, then knelt down beside her.

'Tired Mary, very tired. But I have been thinking. Just thinking back in time love.' She said with a heavy sigh.

'What are your photos, Harriet?' Mary asked picking them up.

Harriet sighed heavily again. She ran bony fingers through her sparse grey hair. 'Just all I have to show for my life really.' And with a shake of her head added. 'Not much is it.'

'Who is this beautiful young woman Harriet, is it you?' The nurse
exclaimed holding up a picture of a lone well dressed teenager. 'Yes it is you, I can see the likeness. Harriet love, you were a real stunner.'

The old lady smiled, her eyes had a far away look. 'I was sixteen then and had gingery fair hair. It was taken before I left Portsmouth.'

'Is this Portsmouth?' Mary asked holding up another photo. 'What a lovely harbour scene. Were you born here Harriet?'

Harriet adjusted herself in her seat and glanced out of the window and watched blackbirds playing on the lawn before answering. 'No, I was born in Aston in Birmingham in 1898.' She hesitated, thinking. 'My father died that same year. Suddenly I think. I don't know how. Mother had a breakdown I was told and had to go and live with her mother, Mary Anne. She took my elder sister Florence with her, but my other sister Nelly and I was sent to stay with my grandmothers sister Harriet, whom I was named after, in Portsmouth. I was just a baby. I don't remember any of that.'

A far away look spread over the tired but once beautiful face as she recalled precious long gone memories.

The nurse left her alone and as she set about putting the clean linen on the bed thought about the horrible start in life for a young girl. The sun was now high in the sky and the breeze getting warmer and stronger, fluttered the pink floral curtains to and fro. Harriet looked round and beckoned to Mary who picked up the only old dining chair and placed it by her easy chair and sat down.

'Would you like to know more Mary?' She whispered as if she was about to reveal a secret. Putting on her glasses she fiddled with her photos and selected the Portsmouth harbour scene again. 'This is where I first remember anything about my life.' A happy look brightened her eyes. 'This is where I spent a happy childhood.' She was silent again as she stared at the scene. Rising stiffly from her chair and with the aid of her walking stick, hobbled over to the window. 'Yes we had great fun staying with Aunt Harriet and Uncle Mike.' She thought for a moment, a bent finger touching her wrinkled forehead.

'He was her second husband, a sailor and great fun. They lived next to Aunt Harriet's son Harry and his wife Louise. They had young children too.'

Harriet paused for a moment and leaning on the window sill breathed in deeply. She turned suddenly as if remembering. 'Do you have time to listen Mary?' A little crooked smile accentuating the wrinkles on her face.

'Yes love. I have plenty of time and I am eager to learn about your time in Portsmouth.' The nurse replied as she gripped her old patients arm and helped her back to her chair. She sank heavily into it. The exercise seem to tire her for she closed her eyes for a moment before continuing. 'Uncle Mike used to take us down to the docks. He played hide and seek with us amongst the tar barrels. Sometimes we would have a picnic by the harbour walls and watch the screeching gulls swooping and diving through the masts and riggings of the old sailing ships.' Her head leaned backwards on her chair and her eyes closed again. ' I can still remember the smell of tar, Mary, the sea air, the sooty smell of the steamers and the noise of ships sirens.'

She stopped again, deep in thought. Mary handed her a glass of water and a pill and watched her as she put it in her mouth and wash it down. After a rest she continued again. 'These were happy days for me Mary, I wanted for nothing. I was spoiled rotten. And especially when my sister Nelly went back to stay with mother in Aston. My mother had remarried and now had a son by her new husband.' She halted briefly. 'Now I had more attention lavished on me and I loved it.' She had a smile on her face as she remembered. 'And when Aunt Harriet's son Harry, left with his family to begin a new life in Scotland I received even more attention. I was made to feel special, extra special. They used to call me their little princess. I am afraid I was a proper snob.'

'Oh I am sure you gave them very much happiness in return, my dear.
After all, you were their little princess remember.' Mary left her to
adjust the curtains as the sun's rays slanted into the room. Somewhere a blackbird struck up a lovely song, serenading its mate. Mary sat down beside Harriet again. 'What happened after that love? I can tell there is a but coming here.' the nurse gently held Harriet's hand.

She nodded her grey haired head slowly, tears welling in her eyes. 'Yes it all came to an end when uncle Mike died suddenly in 1914 just at the beginning of the First World war. After that aunt Harriet was persuaded to go and live in Scotland with her son.' Her eyes closed briefly before she added hurriedly. 'Oh I could have gone too but my mother wanted me to stay with her. I was sixteen. I felt as though my world had ended.'

Harriet fingered the photo of herself, sadly stroking it with a bent finger. 'I used to help my Aunt Harriet in her little shop making cane furniture, which I enjoyed. But staying with my Mother I had to work in a factory. It seemed beneath me. Working in overalls at a milling machine, getting dirty. Big noisy machines, long hours, it was horrible.

I hated it. And to make matters worse I didn't get on with my step-father. I was desperate to get away from it all.'

Mary noticed she was getting agitated. She was twisting her handkerchief in both hands, and she whispered gently. 'Take it easy now love.'

Then Harriet continued angrily. 'Nobody told me they loved me or that I looked nice. No one complimented me for anything that I tried to do. The men I met were so unromantic, unflattering,' she paused before saying softly, 'so when I met Charles he seemed different.' Harriet looked again at the photo of herself. 'He made me feel important, so when he proposed, I accepted. I thought it was an escape. A chance to have a home of my own.' Once more she went quiet. 'Well it was all right for a while, then children came along and although I loved them I sometimes became jealous of them. They were getting more attention than I was.'

Harriet straightened out her twisted handkerchief and dabbed her eyes with it. They kept filling up. Mary adjusted the curtains again.

Somewhere in the garden someone was using a lawnmower and in the distance someone could be heard laughing.

'Do you want to stop for a rest Harriet?' the nurse asked

'No I am all right, besides you haven't heard about America yet.' Her arms were waving in protest.

'It's okay, my dear, I am listening.' Mary hastily sat down again.

'We decided to emigrate to Canada in 1921. The land of opportunity. I thought it romantic at first. But after we had been there for five years I discovered life was just the same there. People were always too busy to notice me. At least that is what I thought.

Then a group of us who had originally came from England decided to move to America. And we all settled in Elyria.' Once again Harriet stopped for a rest. 'Times were tough there and I had to get a job to make ends meet and I really was so exhausted.' As if on cue she halted to catch her

60

breath. Her claw like hand running over her forehead. 'With long hours and hard work I was always too tired to be a wife and mother and consequently I was very often short tempered with the children. I didn't mean to take it out on them but in one incident, in a fit of temper I hurled my son Eric down some stairs and he lost the sight in one eye.'

She sobbed, both her hands covering her face and through them she continued. 'In another fit of temper I poured boiling water over my daughter Georgina, badly scalding her.' When her sobbing subsided she tearfully carried on. 'My husband constantly blamed me. Said I was a useless wife and mother. I was so low, desperate. No one said they loved me. I was so depressed.' Tears were streaming down her face now and her shoulders heaved with each sob.

After a short pause she began again. 'All that happened in the first year in America. Then my friend Alice who had travelled from Canada at the same time as us persuaded me to join the Merry Twelve club. It was a club set up by emigrants from England. Charles would never join these clubs and in a way I was glad about that, because that is where I met George. He was a friend of Alice but Alice wanted him to be more than just a friend.' Harriet's face lit up. 'So when this handsome young immigrant began taking an interest in me, much to the annoyance of Alice, I was flattered. When he began paying me compliments I was delighted.' A smile flickered on her lips as she remembered precious moments. 'We started to see each other secretly. Precious moments Mary. I couldn't get enough of them and of course we took chances.' Harriet covered her face with her hands. 'The arguments between Charles and myself were awful. I hated going home and when he found out about George and I through Alice and her jealousy that was the end. He told me to go.'

Harriet fidgeted in her seat. 'In one way I was glad but I was angry at my friends betrayal and sought revenge on her. What happened next seemed to come quickly one after another. Charles sought a divorce which he got easily. I reported Alice to the authorities for being illegally in America. The papers were full of the story when in the courtroom she attacked and scratched my face after she had been sentenced to be deported back to Canada.'

Harriet hung her head and was silent. Mary touched her arm. 'What happened after that Harriet?'

'Revenge is sweet Mary. Charles discovered that George was in America illegally too and reported him. We were

61

married two days before we boarded the Albertie of the White Star line for our journey back to England.' She paused thinking. 'It should have been a magical trip, with moonlight walks on the decks holding hands, a kiss or two.' She laughed.
'But no it wasn't. Something was different. We both felt it I think.'

A sudden gust of wind caught the curtains and they billowed inwards.
Mary caught them and held them until the breeze softened. Harriet looke as if she appreciated the break, then slowly she continued. 'We settled in Redcar in Yorkshire for a while but the recession made finding work difficult. We grew further apart and one day George disappeared altogether. Rumour had it that he had emigrated to Canada but I never heard from him again. I eventually moved to Aston to be near my sisters.
My life was lonely again and I was still looking for love. Someone to care for me, to make me feel important and special.'

The radio screeched loudly so Mary leaned over and switched it off.
'Noisy thing,' she exclaimed, 'go on dear, what happened next?'

'Oh I was lucky. I applied for a job as a live in housekeeper for wealthy elderly gentleman in Aston, and got it. He was a retired Jeweller. He owned a string of shops all over the country and a factory in Aston. All were by this time, run by his son and daughter. He was good to me. Showered me with lots of gifts and when he gave me jewellery he would say 'beautiful things for a beautiful lady'. He bought me fine clothes. Made me feel like a queen. It was wonderful. I felt really special again.'

Harriet leaned her head back on her chair. Her lined face looked grey and a thin sheen of sweat glistened on her forehead. 'His son started paying me a lot of attention too, Mary. He was married and had a family but he would take me with him on business trips and meet his wealthy friends, wine and dine me. It was all so grand. I felt I had everything, a grand house, security and more important I was loved and adored.
Appreciated. I was able to go and visit friends and family in my finery.
Real fur coats, expensive jewellery, big fancy hats and lovely dresses..
I even had a visit to Scotland to see my relations there and

I would boast about my important position.' Harriet sighed heavily.

'Is there another 'but' coming up here love?' Mary held her hands.

'After many good years with the old gentleman and the adoration lavished by his son, others of his family began to object. But it wasn't until the old man died suddenly one night when he and I were alone in the house, that certain members of the family began to point fingers. I was accused of all sorts of things. The only person that stuck by me was the old gentleman's son, but even then our special relationship was being frowned on, not surprisingly by his wife.'

Wearily she picked up her glasses and her photos and laid them carefully on the little table and turned to face the nurse. 'And that is my story Mary. I was handsomely paid off and for many years lived in comfort. But it is all gone now. Nothing left. Nothing but my memories. My children will all be grown up now. They may have children of their own. I wonder if they ever think of me or talk of me. The mother who abandoned them because she needed more love and attention than them. There is a word for that Mary. I think it is called narcissism.'

Mary helped Harriet into bed. She was exhausted now. 'There now dear you have been up long enough now.' And after seeing she was cosily tucked up, she placed her photos on the bedside cabinet and quietly left.

The following morning Harriet was found to have passed away during the night. In her lifeless hands she held her two photos and on her face was a peaceful smile.

In 2009 Harriet's granddaughter in America, whilst researching her
family history tried to find out something of her grandmother that
nobody ever spoke about.

She found a death certificate dated 1968. Place of death was a
retirement home in Birmingham. Only possessions left-----
One wedding
ring. Whose?

The end.

And now something different. Something silly.

THE BLONDE LADY.

'Drink up Joe and try and calm down.'

'Can't help it. I haven't done this sort of thing before.'

'Relax man. I can't believe you have never been to a convention before.'

'Always went fishing instead, Derek.'

' Look, for tonight ,forget you are a boring old accountant. The Blonde Lady will certainly make you forget.'

'Imagine me on a blind date. What is she like Derek?'

'She is great. Out of this world. And that is where she will take you tonight.'

'If she is that wonderful, why haven't you kept her for yourself?'

'Once only rule, I'm afraid Joe. The Blonde Lady likes variety. Two nights every year, two different men.'

'What number were you Derek?'

'I was the first. Five years ago. Since then I have fixed her up with two men every year. This year you are the lucky man Joe.'

They were standing at the crowded bar of a posh hotel. Joe looked uncomfortable in his evening suit and bow tie. He was about to ask Derek another question when a colleague butted in. 'Hi, Joe, how are you feeling?'

'I am okay Sam. Just a bit nervous and apprehensive.'

'You will be feeling better later, Joe. Let me buy you a whisky. On second thoughts, better make it a pint of lucazade. Your going to need it.'

Sam made to leave. 'I'll send a drink over to you Joe.'
Then he stopped and shouted back.
'She's here. Corner table.' And pointing added. 'Good luck Joe.'
Derek gripped Joe's arm. 'Come on. Your fun starts now.'

'Shouldn't I take the lady a drink?' Joe asked hanging back.

'She will have had enough by now. Come on, bring your own drinks.'

They pushed their way through the crowd. 'There she is, the silvery blonde all on her own.' Derek pushed the reluctant Joe forward.

'Hi there, Lady.' He shouted over the noise in the bar. 'Here is your date for tonight. This is Joe.'

The Blonde Lady looked at Joe. Her bright red lips were framed in a seductive smile. Her false eyelashes fluttered rapidly over grey green eyes that sparkled.

Joe looked closer at her in the lowered lights of the Hotel lounge and blinked, his eyebrows raised and his open mouth sucked in air.

She looked closer at Joe and her expression changed. Her eyes widened, eyebrows arched and a squeal escaped from her pouting mouth and she dropped her drink and stumbled wildly from the table. Her ample breasts bursting out of her low cut dress. The wide flared mini-skirt flapped up to reveal suspenders holding up black nylon stockings on her fat but shapely legs as she tottered on high heels.

'Wow, she's never done that before Joe.' Derek gasped in amazement.

Joe still stood facing the vacant space. A glass in both hands. A shocked look on his cherubic face. He gave himself a shake then tossed a whisky down his throat, stared again and downed the other.

'She was wearing a wig.' He exclaimed, and he burst into a fit of uncontrollable giggles. 'She was wearing a bloody wig.'

'Steady on old boy.' Derek tried to calm him. 'Lots of people wear wigs.'

Joe looked at his puzzled friend and in between heavy heaving laughter.

'You don't understand. For five years I have been going fishing instead of going to the works conventions and my wife has been going to her mother's to stay.'

The giggles started again as he pointed to the door the Blonde Lady had dashed through. 'Or so I thought. Your Blonde Lady, Derek is my wife.'

The end.

And another silly one.

IT STARTED WITH A KISS.

'Where are you going?' He said, staring her in the face as he walked backwards.

'Up the hill.' Her pony tail swung as she nodded upwards.

'Can I come with you?' His smile revealed missing front teeth.

'Yes. What's your name?' Her blue eyes twinkled happily.

'My name's Jack. What's yours?' He fell into step beside her.

'My name is Jill. You are really quite handsome.' she said as she cleaned the thick lenses of her glasses.

'I know.' He agreed, as he smoothed his greasy hair with both hands. 'And you are very pretty.'

'I know.' She replaced her glasses. 'Would you like to carry my pail?'

'Okay. Why are you carrying a pail?'

'To get some water at the top of the hill.'

'A long way to go for water.' He swung the pail as he spoke.

'I know and the hill is very steep.' She wiped her nose on the sleeve of her coat.

'Do you do this often?' He watched her transfixed. 'Going for water I mean.'

'Yes every day. Look we are nearly there.'

'Thank goodness, I am quite exhausted.'

'So am I. Lets sit here for a while.' They both sat on the wall of the well.

'Can I put my arm around you Jill?' His arm was already around her as he asked.

'If you like Jack.' She snuggled against him.

'Hmm. You smell nice, can I kiss you Jill?'

She wiped her nose again, on his shirt sleeve. 'Yes if you like Jack.'

They kissed and then they kissed again and then again.

'That was nice Jill, could we----?' He was holding her very tight.

'We had better fill the pail with water first Jack.' She pushed him away.

'Oh very well then.' Jack drew water from the well and filled her pail.

'Now can we kiss again?' His lips were puckered and he bent forward to grab her.

'Okay. Careful you don't spill the water Jack.'

'Damn the water, just come here girl.' He grabbed at her.

'Jack don't do that.' There was a loud slap and Jack let out a yell.

'You little minx.' The side of Jack's face glowed red.
'I know what you need.'
And he dashed at Jill, arms stretched out to grasp her.

Jill caught his arm and swung round and threw him over her shoulder in a neat Judo move and he rolled on and on down the hill, Jill off balance tumbled after him.

At the bottom of the hill Jack groaned and held his head.

'How are you Jill?' He tried to focus his eyes through a fuzzy haze. 'I think I've broke my head.'

Jill stood up and wiped her nose on her sleeve before replying. 'I'm all right Jack.'

68

Then she picked up her pail and set off up the hill again.

A new catch phrase was born that day----'I'm all right Jack.' and all it started with a kiss.

Do you believe that?
                    The End.

So they tell us that Jack and Jill went up the hill to get a pail of water.

Okay. But why did Jack fall down and break his crown?

Well you know now.

And could that selfish little bitch care about his injuries?

No way. All she thought about was herself/

I'm all right Jack.

.

##

THE SHOPKEPER.

The elderly shopkeeper leaned over placing carefully a sweet laden tray onto a window shelf. Proudly he stuck a 'Home Made' notice behind it. The smile on his be-whiskered face turned to scowl when a small ferret faced man in a black pin striped suit on the other side of the window stood shaking his bowler covered head.

'What does that daft beggar want now?' He growled tugging his white apron down over his ample stomach and squaring his white hat securely on his balding head, prepared for battle with his Food Inspector friend.

Before the shop door had time to shut behind him the briefcase holding man, fiercely pointing to the window officially exclaimed. 'You cannot sell these without a health warning.'

The bewildered shopkeeper gasped. 'But I've been selling these for years. Never needed a health warning before.'

'You need one now.' The food inspector said abruptly.

The old man shook his head, puzzled. 'No one has ever suffered through eating my---'

'I don't care, you still need to display a health warning.' The shopkeeper was loudly and rudely cut off by the excitable little man.

'Don't you dare raise your voice to me, little man.' The shopkeepers moustache bristled in anger.' Or I'll throw you out.''I am just making you aware of the law sir.' The Inspector said calmly waving a leaflet in the irate shopkeeper's face. 'You must be aware of the law.'

The old man, in frustration snatched the offending paper from him and scrunching it up threw it away. 'Damn daft laws if you ask me. Making out people are idiots.'

An officious finger pointed in his direction. 'The laws are to protect people from unnecessary accidents or illnesses.'

The angry shopkeeper stamped his feet loudly on the white tiled floor and slapped the counter top in frustration. 'No one has ever suffered an accident or illness from eating my products. I make them myself. They are perfectly safe.'

'Can't help it, it is the law and you must warn people who suffer from a nut allergy.'

The inspector waved a notice with the words, 'Contains Nuts'.

'You daft beggar,' roared the old man snatching his hat from his head and hurling it at the object of his wrath, 'who is going to buy my 'Nutty Toffee bars' if they already know they suffer from a nut allergy?'

The inspector calmly returned the shopkeepers hat. 'There now Albert, you must watch your blood pressure.'

'Honestly, Cyril you do get me going with your daft laws.' Albert wiped the perspiration from his face on his apron. 'Someone should stick a health warning on you.'

Cyril chuckled. 'Only doing my job brother, only doing my job.' And pointing to the window added. 'I'll have my usual please Albert.'

Albert now fully composed, scooped some nutty toffee pieces into a paper bag and passed them over the counter to his brother Cyril. 'I've got to warn you. There are nuts in my toffees.'

The end.

A little tale with a twist.-----

ANGELA'S FIRST DAY AT WORK.

When Angela first entered the door into the factory all eyes turned to stare at her.

There she stood, glancing nervously around her, not at first at her new workmates but more at the lines of big complicated machines that lined the long passageway before her. Her nose screwed up at the strong cloying smell of machine oil.

At first impression she did not look like a factory worker. A second impression wouldn't make you change your mind either. Her long fair hair was tied back tightly in a pony tail. That was okay, but as she cast her blue eyes over the curious blue overall clad girls gathering before her, her eyelashes struggled to flicker because of the thick mascara that clung to them.

'Hi! I'm Angela.' Her voice was husky, as if nervous, almost sexy. She said this as she walked towards the only man present, with her hand outstretched.

He watched, open mouthed as she approached, well glided, her red mini skirt ever shorter with each step, revealing long shapely black stocking clad legs. His eyes were then further distracted by the cleavage that topped an ample bust that was trying to squeeze out of a tight fitting white low cut top. The sweet pungent aroma of expensive perfume attacked his nostrils as she gazed seductively into his eyes. 'I'm here to learn to be a machinist.' The voice was like velvet, soft. Just like the lightly tanned skin that adorned her pretty oval shaped face. 'I'm a bit nervous. I've never operated a machine before.' She smiled revealing even white teeth framed by shapely very red lips.

'Are you sure you have come to the right place Angela?' A tubby little woman wearing a blue cap on her head inquired. Her pale wrinkled face showing some concern.

The man, still staring and open mouthed, eyes popping, said nothing. The other girls gathered round. 'You look like a model, love, what are you doing here?'

Another one spoke as she eyed up Angela. 'You will get sore feet standing at the machines all day in those shoes girl,'

A tall slim kindly faced woman chipped in referring to Angela's red, very high heeled expensive looking shoes that matched her red very expensive handbag that hung from her suntanned arm. 'Could you not get a job as a model then love?'

A question from someone else in the gathering crowd. 'Never tried that.' Angela looked puzzled. 'Where would I see about that?' She added.

'Who sent you here Angela?' A bossy looking woman asked, hands on hips. Looking her up and down, noting her tall shapely figure.

Angela looked at her well manicured hands as she answered. 'The people at the job place.' Then looking at the others, she laughed innocently as she added. 'They said I was too thick for an office job.'

'They actually said you were too thick?' A kindly faced motherly type inquired. 'That wasn't very nice of them. Not very nice at all.'

'Well they didn't actually say that in so many words.' Angela confessed. 'But they hinted pretty well. Anyway other people have said I am thick, even my Dad.'

'One of the girls will take you to get some work clothes, Angela.' The man had apparently found his voice at last. 'Then I will show you your machine.'

One of the girls took Angela by the arm. 'Come with me love, I'll get you fixed up.'

Once gone, the others gathered round the man. One shouted. 'Are they suggesting that we factory workers are stupid?' Another chipped in. 'Is Angela going to get special treatment boss?'

'Nope, she is just another machinist as far as I am concerned.' The boss replied. 'Hah, we'll see.' Came the sarcastic reply. 'A classy looking girl like that will twist you round her little finger.' The other girls loudly agreed.

When Angela returned she looked entirely different. A blue hat was plonked rakishly on her head. Her pony tail sneaking out the back of it. The straight blue overall hid all her beautiful figure, a pair of safety gloves protected her over long nails. She still wore her red high heeled shoes. And when she spoke, it was as if she had been given a factory voice as well. 'What the hell do I look like in this lot.' She moaned.

'You look just just fine love, just fine.' Came the soothing reply from her new workmate.

'Come with me Angela, I'll show you to your machine.' The man said. Angela teetering behind him said to herself in a quiet voice. 'Where have I seen him before?'

He halted at a machine that was in a corner by itself. 'This is the learners machine.' He growled gruffly. And standing behind her, went through the motions of pointing out various parts, what they did and what to watch out for. She nodded several times as if understanding but looked bored. Finally he put his mouth to her ear and whispered. 'What's going on Angela, what are you doing here?'

'What do you mean?' Her voice was husky again, her big blue eyes squinting to look at him.

'I know who you are Angela, what little game are you playing?'

'How do you know me?' She looked at him, an impish smile on her face.

'We have met before Angela. Don't you remember? Or were you too drunk?'

Her blue eyes twinkled as she scanned his face. 'Ah yes. Andy isn't it? The Traders ball, wasn't it?' A dreamy expression clouding her eyes.

'Yes, that is right Angela. Now tell me, why would my boss, Mr Jones, send his beautiful daughter to work in one of his dirty factories? Are you here to spy for him?'

Angela placed her hands on his chest and leaned against him, face tilted, eyes pleading.

'He doesn't know I am here Andy.' Her voice purred. 'He has been impossible to live with since my Mum left him.' Her eyelashes fluttered, a tear clinging to them. 'He told me that I am so useless, that even he, would not give me a job in one of his factories. He also said to look for my Mum and go stay with her.' This time more tears dangled from the thick mascara. 'I don't know

where my Mum is Andy. You won't tell him I am here. Will you Andy?'

Andy chuckled loudly, and holding her by the shoulders smiled widely as he replied.

'I won't, if you don't tell him where your Mum is. It looks like you will be living with me now Angela. And your Mum.'

The end.

What are you after son?-----

FOR YOUR SAKE MUM.

He waited until she was comfortably seated in her big old overstuffed winged red velvet armchair. Then he pushed the wheeled trolley table with a teapot, two cups and a plate of biscuits in front of her before sitting down on a stool by her side.

'This is the retirement home that Mary's mother has moved into.' Her son John said, showing his Mum a big thick glossy magazine containing coloured pictures of new stately buildings. 'She thinks it is great. Wished she had moved in years ago.'

'Oh very nice dear.' She replied glancing quickly at it. 'It looks very comfortable.'

'Yes it is Mum. You should think about something like this.' John went on. 'You are getting on a bit you know.'

'Don't keep reminding me son.' She smilingly said. 'But I am okay. I am still fairly fit'

'I know Mum, you are quite wonderful for your age, but this old house is a bit big for you now.' He persisted. 'Don't you think?'

She tilted her grey haired head to look at him. 'I like my old house John. It contains a lot of memories for me.'

'I know Mum, but just think, a nice little apartment in a modern building surrounded by lush gardens. Less work, nice walks and people your own age around you.' Her son tried hard to convince her, pointing to the photo of the

81

retirement home.

With a sigh of impatience she tried to explain. 'I said it was very nice John. But why should I leave here? I am quite happy here in my old house.'

'But Mum, just think, you would get a good price for this house. In fact I already know someone who would love to buy it.' He was pleading now.

'What would I do with all that money? I am quite comfortable as I am John.' She teased as she lifted the teapot.

He angrily rattled the teacups together. 'Mum don't just keep thinking of yourself. Settled in a nice compartment like that I wouldn't need to worry so much about you. Her son protested.

For a moment his mother looked slightly miffed before she exclaimed dramatically. 'You will not need to worry about me when I get married John.' She had a big grin on her face as she poured tea into the cups.

John let the biscuits slide off the plate he was picking up. 'Married? What do you mean, getting married?'

'Yes, married John, that is what I said. You know, when a man and a woman say 'I do' at a wedding. That sort of married.' His mother was looking serious now.

'But Mum, who? I didn't know there was anybody.' Her son was searching for the right words.

'Well you don't visit very often to find these things out, do you?' She replied tritely.

'Who is this man?' John said angrily. 'Is it someone after your money?'

She thought for a moment. 'Maybe.' She muttered quietly, thinking. 'He is a lot younger than me.'

'What.' His face was red and he was spluttering, 'What are you thinking of Mother? A younger man?' John was struggling now. 'You can't.'

'Yes I can.' She quickly and angrily cut him off. 'I am old enough to know what I am doing.'

'That's the point Mum. Your age.' John was quite white faced now. 'You can't be serious. I can't believe it.' His mouth was open and he was shaking his head in unbelief.

His mother stared at him with a stern look for a minute before she started wriggling about in her chair and then burst into a fit of giggles. 'Oh John, it is always so easy to wind you up. Who would want to marry a cantankerous old fool like me?' She wheezed as she wiped her eyes with a tissue.'

Her son looked at the biscuit he had crumbled unconsciously in his hand and shook his head. She had done it again. Of all the mothers in the world, he had to get the one who was the best at winding people up. Especially him.

Controlling her giggles she announced in a firm voice. 'I have already sold the house and I move into that same retirement home as Mary's Mum next month.' And then she started giggling again. 'I was going to tell you John.'

John just stared, afraid to say anything more in case it was all another wind up.   THE END.

And now two very short stories depicting differing thoughts about the popular sport of Skiing.

THE SKI SLOPES, YES!

The call of the wilderness of the snow clad mountain tops has always beckoned me.

It is an escape from the ties of responsibilities. The peace and quiet that echo's from peak to peak. The smell of pine from the mountainside firs drifting on the keen fresh air.

These things to me spell the word, 'Skiing'. Wonderful.

The excitement for me begins the moment I escape from the jungles of town life. The journey north to the Ski slopes of Aviemore. Skis firmly attached to the car roof rack.

When I am asked why I get so excited about skiing, my answer is always the same. The anticipation begins first with the planning. Dates, booking, all the necessary little things needed to make a trouble free holiday. First the preparation, then the arrival. The first sight of the ski slopes starts the shivers of excitement up and down my spine.

Then there is the ski clothes. The sleek designs immediately transports me into the champions league. The smell of ski clothes to me is appetising. If they were sweets they would be cool fresh mints.

Waiting for the ski lift to carry me up the steep mountain side sets my heart pounding. The slow journey up gives me time to take in the panoramic view of the peaks and slopes of the snow clad resort. A clear blue sky dotted with floating fluffy cotton buds.

At the top, the tingling fresh air burns into your lungs driving out all the impurities of city life. The occasional smell of smoke from wood burning fires drifting upwards tickles my nostrils.

The spurts of powdered snow as the skier in front launches himself away.

The view from the starting point, gazing down onto a shining glassy slope worked flat by countless previous skiers.   And now the way is clear. All eyes are focussed on me. My figure hugging ski suit showing off all my womanly attributes. It is my turn.

Glasses down, protection from the sun's reflection on the alabaster surface. Knees bent at the right angle. Lean forward, a push and I am off. Racing down the hillside all my tensions ease away. The icy blast numbs my cheeks. The blurred figures of spectators are left behind as I fly. The smooth rasping noise of ski on snow is music to my ears. At that moment the slope is my lover, transporting me to heights no man could ever hope to achieve. A yell. Then it is all over. The climax is reached as I slither to a stop, my legs trembling my head buzzing.

Next time it will be even better I promise myself.

THE END.

THE SKI SLOPES. OH NO.

The reservation was made for me. A weekend break in a comfortable Highland Hotel.

Lovely! Destination Aviemore. Oh no, the ski slopes. I hate the ski slopes. The very words sends shivers down my spine.

'Oh you will love it.' Was the response to my wail of dismay. 'Just think of the clean fresh air.'

Oh I like fresh air. But mountain fresh is a bit too strong for my constitution. My lungs prefer the quality of the lower down stuff.

'The exercise will do you good as well.' She still tried to persuade me of the benefits of a skiing holiday. 'Help you lose weight too.'

Exercise and weight are two words I never use together, unless it is exercising my arm lifting a heavy steak sandwich.

'Yes all that tramping up and down the slopes will do you the world of good darling.' She tried hard to convince. 'No way.' I protested. 'probably end up with pneumonia.'

'Nonsense.' She always seemed to know better. 'The bracing mountain breeze and the strong winter sun is what you need to make you feel alive.'

'I prefer to feel alive in front of a nice big log fire,' I tried hard to reason with her.

'We may even tempt you on to skis as well dear.' Now she was going too far.

'No way.' I protested. 'Coming here with you is

one thing, joining you on the slopes is another.'

I didn't have the nerve to tell her how much I hated these skiing weekends. The mountains depressed me. I was always miserable just hanging about, waiting. I could never see the pleasure in waiting for the ski lift that slowly and monotonously dragged you up the hillside to the starting point. And that mad downwards rush, yes that crazy dash down that white glassy slope was, well, just madness in my opinion. It took longer to go up than it did to come down. A total waste of time was my verdict.

But my dear wife thought it was the best thing in the world. In fact she constantly raved about skiing to all who would listen. I must admit though, there is one thing I enjoy about her sport and that is her figure hugging ski outfits. She always looks terrific in them.

Will I be accompanying her on her next skiing weekend?

You bet. It is cheaper than a divorce.

THE END.

A little tale of observation.

THE DINING ROOM.

Imagine the scene in the dining room of the classic Castle Hotel. Rows of tables regimentally placed are all set precisely for four people. White coated waiters glide silently over the thick blue carpet from their sideboard, neatly laid out with plates, dishes, glasses and cutlery and menu cards and wine lists. To the side of that is the door to the kitchen from where the many appetising smells of cooking emanate. On the other side of the sideboard is the door that leads to the Foyer and beside that stands two tall coat stands. All is silent in the room.

At a table to the right of a heavy curtained window and in a corner, an elderly couple was seated. Before them was untouched drinks and when they spoke they did so in whispers, as if afraid of breaking the silence of a holy place.

In the left corner, a tall prim looking woman sat. Her brown two piece suit and white polo necked jumper, from which a long neck protruded supporting a long unsmiling face topped off with very short greying hair that gave her a severe school mistress look.

The only thing that tried to soften her looks was a red rose that was pinned to her right lapel. Her staring eyes were fixed on the swing doors, as if she was expecting someone.

Also on the left at a table near her, a small blue suited man was nervously playing with his yellow bow tie and patting his dyed black oil slicked hair. On the opposite wall four well dressed business men shared a table. Not speaking, just looking through their menus. Next to them, near the kitchen door, almost hidden from view, a grey haired old man sat all on his own, eyes staring at nothing in particular.

Sitting at a table near the swing doors was a casually dressed middle aged couple. They looked as if they could have been reliving some past happy occasion for they whispered and smiled and touched each others hands and stared lovingly into each others eyes.

No one paid any attention when two waiters began qui placing two tables together in front of the windows and setting them for six.

The atmosphere of the place was reserved with a silence that was not to be broken. The elderly couple glanced shyly around them, clearly uncomfortable. The business men began chatting in hushed tones. The lone elderly man still stared into space, perhaps he was reliving some special time at this same table. The severe looking woman still stared at the swing doors. The nervous man looked even more nervous as he picked up and laid down his menu. The casually dressed couple still touched hands and smiled lovingly at each other, eyes locked on eyes. All was set for a quiet peaceful meal.

Suddenly the swing doors burst open. A group of laughing people surged in headed by a giant of a man dressed in a light grey suit, blue shirt and an enormous pink tie. Loud it advertised and loud he was. His whole demeanour shouted--'look at me'.

'Hi, waiter, mister Biggens, table for six.' His voice boomed.

The elderly couple looked horrified. That somebody should dare desecrate the sanctity of this majestic place was written all over their faces.. The business men glanced up and then down, slightly shaking their heads. The severe looking woman had a look of annoyance on her face. The nervous man twitched more. The casual couple sniggered, hands still on hands, eyes still on eyes. The elderly man still stared, at nothing.

The waiter led the group to their table set for six. 'Champagne waiter. The best in the house.' The voice of the giant boomed again. Then seeing that everyone was seated he looked around as if he was going to make a speech. And he was. 'Folks it's my twenty fifth wedding anniversary today and I want you all to join me in a toast.' He stopped and guffawed loudly. 'Sorry I got that wrong. My wife is twenty five and this is our first anniversary.' His table guests roared with laughter. One shouted. 'Good one Elvis.'

The group all clapped and cheered noisily. 'Waiter.' The voice boomed again. 'Champagne for every one if you please.'

The elderly couple tried to shrink further into their corner. The business men all nodded their thanks. The severe lady looked horrified. The nervous man twitched. The casual couple smiled their thanks. The old man just stared.

Just then a young couple floated in. They held on to each other as if they were afraid to let go in case one of them might float away. The kissed, rubbed noses and coo'd, just as the young and in love do. The waiter had to guide them to their table by the coat stand. There they collapsed into each others arms and stayed there.

The elderly couple shook their heads. The business men glanced and sniggered. The stern woman looked horrified again, the nervous man tried to hide behind a menu and the casual couple sighed. The old man still just stared.

The din of the party got louder, the shrieks and laughter assaulted the reserve of the setting as the diners began their first course. No one seemed to notice a swing door partly open and a plain dark straggly haired, worried looking face of a young woman peered round. Slowly she edged her way in, shyly looking around, not seeing who she was to meet.

All eyes, except the party group was looking at her now, wondering.

The stern lady half stood up, staring, fingers on her rose bearing lapel.

The nervous man stopped being nervous and straightened his bow tie.

The old couple stared, open mouthed.

The casual couple, like the couple in love by the coat stand didn't notice. They were too preoccupied.

The business men were side glancing, smirking, taking bets with each other.

After hesitating again and trying to smooth her crumple green dress she looked pleadingly at the waiter who listened to her for a moment and then beckoned her to follow him.

The stern lady began to smile. The nervous man began to smile.

As the girl approached the table she hesitated before saying quietly. 'Hello Dad. I am home.-----to stay.'

Tears ran down from the old man's unseeing eyes as he held out welcoming arms.

THE END.

I hope you have enjoyed reading
These mixed bag of short stories.

M.POULSON-FERGUSON.

8513235R0

Made in the USA
Charleston, SC
17 June 2011